MARGRET & H. A

Curious George

Goes to a Chocolate Factory

WALKER BOOKS

AND SUBSIDIARIES

LONDON · BOSTON · SYDNEY · AUCKLAND

First published in Great Britain 2006
by Walker Books Ltd, 87 Vauxhall Walk, London SE11 5HJ

6 8 10 9 7

© 1998 Houghton Mifflin Company
Curious George® is a registered trademark of Houghton Mifflin Company
Published by arrangement with Houghton Mifflin Company

This book has been typeset in Gill Sans MT Schoolbook
Illustrated in the style of H. A. Rey by Vipah Interactive

Printed in China

British Library Cataloguing in Publication Data:
a catalogue record for this book is available from the British Library

ISBN 978-1-4063-0038-3

www.walker.co.uk

This is George.

George was a good little monkey and always very curious. One day George went for a drive with his friend, the man with the yellow hat.

"Look, George," the man said. "There's a shop in that chocolate factory up ahead. Let's stop for a treat."

George loved chocolates.
Inside the shop, boxes of chocolates
were stacked everywhere, but the man
with the yellow hat found his favourites
straight away. "George," he said,
"wait here while I buy these,
and please stay out of trouble."

George looked around the shop.

He saw chocolate-covered cherries

and fudge-flavoured lollipops.

A chocolate bunny caught his eye.

Then something else caught his eye.

What were all those people looking at?

George was curious.

He climbed up to get
a better look. Through
the window he saw lots
of trays filled with little
brown dots.
What were all those
little brown dots?

George was curious.
He found a door that led
to the other side of the window.

The little brown dots were chocolates, of course! A tour guide was showing a group of people how to tell what was inside the chocolates by looking at the swirls on top.

This little swirl means fudge,	this one says that caramel is inside	and this wiggle is for marshmallow.

This is the squiggle for a truffle,	this one is for nougat,	this sideways swirl is for orange fluff

and this one is for George's favourite – banana cream.

George followed the tour group until they came to a balcony overlooking a room where the chocolates were made. Down below, busy workers picked the sweets off the machines and put them in boxes.

SLOW
MEDIUM
FAST
EXTRA FAST

These were the machines that made the chocolates with the swirls on top! The chocolates came out of the machines on long belts. But how did they get their swirls? George was curious.

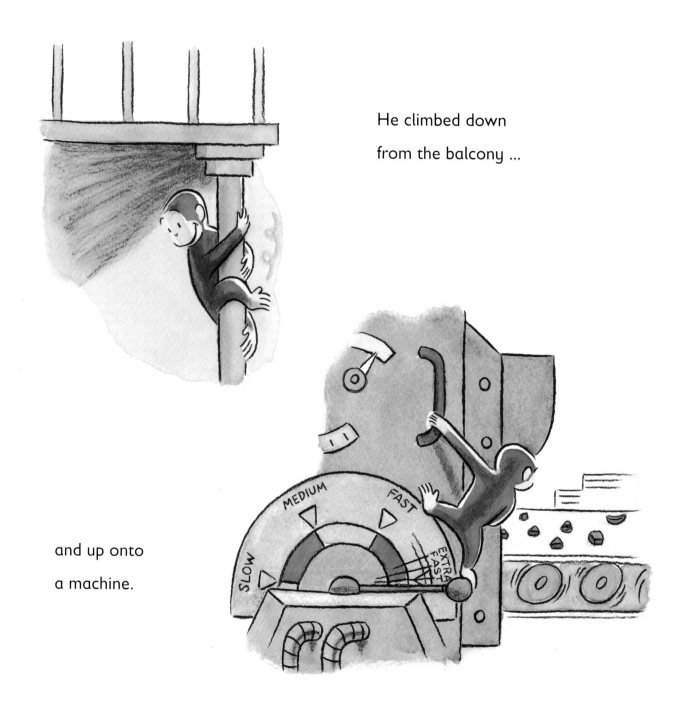

He climbed down
from the balcony ...

and up onto
a machine.

SLOW MEDIUM FAST EXTRA FAST

14

George peeked inside.
He was trying to see what
was making the swirls when
all of a sudden ...

the chocolates began
coming out faster and faster!
They sped by him so quickly
they seemed to be running
on legs of their own.

16

"Quick! Bring more boxes!" yelled a man with a tall white hat. "What happened?" asked another man. Nobody answered. Nobody knew what had happened and everyone was so busy that no one noticed George.

The workers began to fall behind and the sweets began to fall off the end of the belt.

"Save the chocolates!" yelled the man with the tall white hat.

Meanwhile, George saw one of his favourites whizz by.

He tried to catch the banana-cream chocolate,

but it was too fast!

He chased it to the end of the belt.

At the end of the belt a pile of chocolates was growing taller and taller. George had never seen so many chocolates! As he searched for the banana cream, he put the others in empty boxes.

George was a fast worker. Someone noticed and yelled,
"Bring that monkey more boxes! He's helping us catch up!"

Not all the chocolates made it into boxes,

but no more chocolates fell on the floor.

Just when George and the workers were all caught up, the tour guide ran in with the man with the yellow hat. "Get that monkey out of here!" she yelled. "He's ruining our chocolates!"

"But this little monkey SAVED the chocolates," explained the workers.

Then the man with the tall white hat said to George, "You may have caused us some trouble, but you were a speedy little monkey. You deserve a big box of chocolates for all your help." George was glad he was not in trouble, but he did not take the chocolates.

Back in the car park, the workers waved good-bye
as George and his friend got into their little blue car.
"George, are you sure you don't want any chocolates
before we leave?" asked the man with the yellow hat.

George was sure.